The Princess and the Presents

For Mum
C.H.

For Lee, just for everything
S.W.

First published in 2014 by Nosy Crow Ltd
The Crow's Nest, 10a Lant Street
London SE1 1QR
www.nosycrow.com

ISBN 978 0 85763 302 6

Nosy Crow and associated logos are trademarks
and/or registered trademarks of Nosy Crow Ltd.

A CIP catalogue record for this book is available from the British Library.

Printed in China
Papers used by Nosy Crow are made from
wood grown in sustainable forests.

1 3 5 7 9 8 6 4 2

The Princess

and the

Presents

Caryl Hart

Sarah Warburton

nosy crow

"It's Princess Ruby's birthday soon,"
The king cried, in a tizzy.
He put the maids in such a whirl,
It made the footmen dizzy.

The people up and down the land
Were making preparations,
Baking cakes and puddings
For the coming celebrations.

High up in the tower
Little Ruby lounged in bed.
"My special day must be the BEST
Or else!" the princess said.

She shouted out her orders,
While the servants bowed and smiled.

She yelled and bawled
and kicked her feet.
She was a horrid child.

"I WANT a giant tree house
AND a parrot that can talk.

Bye!

I WANT a pair of fancy shoes
That light up when I walk.

Monday
Tuesday
Wednesday
Thursday
Friday

I NEED a new tiara
To wear each day at school.

AND a pony AND some roller skates
And LOADS and LOADS of jewels.

I WANT a massive birthday feast
With sweets and posh ice cream . . .

Or I'll lie down on the palace floor
And scream and scream and . . .

SCREAM!"

"Of course, my darling," soothed the king,
And down the stairs he dashed.
He rushed out to the high street
With a great big case of cash.

He chose the very nicest things
That royal coins could get,
To make sure Ruby's special day
Would be the best one yet.

The birds were singing in the trees.
The day was warm and clear.

"I WANT MY PRESENTS!"
Ruby yelled, and shoved her dad aside.

The king woke up his daughter,

Singing, "HAPPY BIRTHDAY, dear!"

She ran down to the ballroom
And this is what she spied . . .

She grabbed the biggest gift of all.
She didn't even smile.
She ripped the pretty paper off
And tossed it in a pile.

"BUT WHERE'S MY GIANT TREE HOUSE?"
Bawled the greedy little tyke.
"You promised me a mobile phone,
THREE puppies AND a bike!"

"There, there, my dear," replied the king.
He opened up the door . . .

The servants heaved MORE parcels in
And heaped them on the floor.

They piled the gifts and presents
On the tables and the chairs.

They built them into towers
Up and down the palace stairs.

They filled up all the bedrooms
And the bathrooms and the halls.

There were presents in the kitchen
And stacked up against the walls.

"This is more like it," Ruby scowled.
"It's just what I deserve.
I'll open all my presents
Then my banquet can be served."

But . . .

. . . as she spoke there came a crash. The ceiling bowed and groaned.
Great cracks appeared in all the walls. "What NOW?" the princess moaned.
"I've bought too many heavy things!" the worried king replied.
"THE PALACE IS COLLAPSING!
Ruby, quickly! RUN OUTSIDE!"

"But what about my brand-new stuff?" The selfish princess whined.
"Go and save it NOW.
And don't leave ANYTHING behind!"
The brave king raced along the hall, dodging falling plaster.
Then with a groan, the roof caved in . . .

. . . a terrible disaster!

"What HAVE I done?" sobbed Ruby.
"The best thing I ever had
Is buried in a pile of bricks.
PLEASE! Help me save . . .

. . . my DAD!

Those gifts are less important than the person I ADORE.
I'd give up ALL these presents just to see my dad once more."

The fire brigade sent out the word,
"His Highness is in trouble!"
Kind people came from far and wide
To search beneath the rubble.

After hours and hours of digging
They heard some quiet knocks . . .

sniff
sniff

. . . and found His Royal Highness safe
Inside a cardboard box!

"My darling little Ruby,
I'm SO sorry," sighed the king.
"Your birthday's wrecked. Your home is gone.
I've ruined everything."

"MY DADDY!" Ruby shouted.
"All I really want is YOU.
I realise I've been selfish
And I know just what to do.

"We'll build the little tree house
And line the floor with rugs.
This piece of cake is still OK
And, look, I've found some mugs."

Then she made the helpful people
A delicious picnic tea . . .

. . . and lived happily for ever
With her daddy in a tree.

THE END!